Phenomenal Lover

By Christopher W. Strahan
-Poetic Storm-

Published By Writing in Faith
IAmWritingInFaith. com

Cover Design By
Christopher Strahan Christopher Strahan (Text)
ISBN 13: 979-8-9889051-1-0

Table of Contents

Acknowledgements

There are countless people I would like to thank for their help throughout my life. Without them I would not be who I am, nor would I be doing what I do. For the sake of brevity here, I would like to thank God for the people He has placed in my life for this season, to help me with the success of this book.

First, I thank those of you that have supported me through the venture of pre-ordering my book, I know it has been a long time coming, but with the help of a close friend and sponsor, Phenomenal Lover has taken flight and has now landed into your reading eyes and listening ears.

Thank you, Mom, and Dad. Without your unconditional support this book would never have come to be.

Thank you, Ericka "Lady T" Taylor, for pushing this idea through while we were sitting in the radio studio on the airwaves of WABL 1570 AM and 93.7 FM in Amite, LA.

Thank you, Minister Tiffany Lee of New Orleans, LA for being one of the most thoughtful, loving, kind-hearted and generous people I know. You encouraged me to keep pushing this book until it was completed, as well as sponsored me in getting it launched.

Thank you, Kenya Harris of Writing in Faith. You're the most patient and understanding publisher I know, and you have been very instrumental in helping me start and launch my writing career.

Poetic Pieces

The Essence of Her

The Bible speaks of the marriage bed being honorable and undefiled. Since this statement reaches deep within the veins of my soul like the blood that gives me life, it makes me know how I'm going to love you.

I want you in ways that will put you into outer body experiences. I have imagined us in places other than our residence with me doing things to you that you have fantasized about doing to me.

I know within you, my favor, my good thing,

has launched a new revelation in my love life writing a new true novel, that couples will go into new worlds of paradise in dimensions where only their love is birthed.

They dance and sway with one another and the equally yoked vibrations they have for one another creating colors, waiting to be used on parchment drawn on a canvas that rejuvenates all marriages.

I do want to know how much you love me. I want to always look into your eyes and see our fantasy created each day when we cross in thoughts daydreaming for one another.

You send my energy to the next level of universes that are yet waiting to be discovered by earthly scientists. I think of you every jiffy within a second lost in the true essence of time.

You are my dream girl that was formed in my thoughts when I was an embryo to be manifested at this junction in time. I love you my butterfly with every beat of my heart, when it beats, it creates a new melody for you unheard by the world.

- Poetic Storm (Christopher W. Strahan)

Thoughts of Her

I thought that I'd seen beauty in my imagination When I heard the words of Amazing Grace,

I thought that I'd known love,

But it was embedded in your heart for me when I gazed upon your face.

I thought I'd felt my heartbeat to the beat of your soul, I tried to dance but my knees were weak.

You were the most beautiful songbird singing to my heart, your voice is like a melody when I hear you speak.

I thought the rose was fragrant I thought the sky was blue,

I thought nature wonderful,

But not until I first laid eyes on you.

I thought the sun was shining I thought I'd seen it all,

I thought that I was standing strong, but your illuminated radiant glow made me fall.

Fainted and landing on clouds created by love, I knew that GOD made you from my desires found only above.

I thought my eyes were open Yet now I'm not so sure,

I think that I may be in love Like I've never loved before.

I'll hold on to these feelings and keep them safe within,

Until the time they're needed, and true love can begin...

~Poetic Storm (Christopher W. Strahan)

My Forever Symphony

She plays on the strings of my heart. Oh, how you can hear the sound of many symphonies soothing the hearts of many others, from the energy of her love for me -- longing to hold their love close, deep within never losing focus on what brought them together!

GOD has created you for me I know, the very moment you existed it gave my heart life. As you begin to grow silent, I know you hear how my soul is moving through multiple universes finding your light through a special star that twinkles.

It shines the glow of how I loved you before we came through the birth canal of our mother's wombs.

I loved you already -- My Summer Rain, My Beautiful Butterfly, My Amazing Help Meet, as we soar through the atmosphere the very depths of our DNA connected, finding one another, grasping, looking, as our eyes pierce into our souls. We know that our eyes are the windows to our own world created by the love we will share forever.

I'll Always Love You Infinity My Butterfly/Summer Rain.

~ Poetic Storm (Christopher W. Strahan

My Hidden Heart

Craving to see her, touch her, hold her, to caress her warm embrace. Wanting to feel her soul dance excitedly next to mine beyond the endless moonlight.

Where can she be? She's taken my heart and hidden it deep within her, never letting go; she keeps it where it's never to be found by any other's woman love but hers.

She protects it, making it only beat for her, because she knows she holds the life force of it, and it only lives because of her nourishment.

Doesn't she know without her energy flowing through its veins that it will cease to exist? Only her frequency can support the life force it gives, keeping it pulsating continuously through dimensions unknown.

Whatever you do, promise me, you'll always continue to nourish, protect the love it has for you. It only lives for infinity because of the love GOD has placed in it for you.

You will Always Be My Love, MY Butterfly, My

Summer Rain

~Poetic Storm (Christopher W. Strahan)

You Deserve the Best

My Butterfly, My Heartbeat.

How you make me weak in the knees.

To gaze at you hanging high up there

in the blissful night sky.

How do you think the stars shine enviously?

Your aura shines the path to the most amazing love that
showers over my soul,

connecting through this earthly realm,

before the dinosaurs set foot upon the magnificent soil.

When the sun rises in the sky,

It reminds me of the radiant light you give to me
which causes me to glow each day, floating through the
atmosphere each hour.

It's when I come out late at night, and I feel alone, I
know you are there, weightless over me.

I know because of my shortness of breath, tells me that
during the infamous day how I miss you.

Every time I blink, I can feel you walking through my
thoughts, missing me too, to hold you, to crave you, to
touch you, passionately,

with the tune of your energy as I play deeply on the
emotional strings of your heart.

It vibrates for me infinity like tidal waves on the ocean

going back and forth soothing the sands of the shores on the beach.

You deserve the very best, a man that will back you up without limits, let you grow without borders and love you without end.

I will always treat you as my favor, my good thing, as GOD sees us both giving us a beautiful grand expected end.

We are one another's rib, flesh of my flesh bone of my bone, as we walk this path of life without fear of infidelity, knowing we are equally yoked, kindred spirits, immaculate vibes created by the

MOST HIGH, never fading into darkness, and never causing a rift between us.

I will always carry you in my spirit allowing our love to be seen from the inside out.

~Poetic Storm (Christopher W. Strahan)

Pure Ecstasy is Her Name

I gazed into her eyes, such a beautiful brown. My heart whispered to me, that energy is right and very profound. Waves ceased crashing; the earth stood still for a brief second and rotated backwards in time. That's where my imagination and desire saw the sweet silhouette of her figure dancing gloriously in my mind. As the Infallible WORD OF GOD states pray without ceasing, I prayed you down from the third Heaven before we knew one other on earth, we knew and loved one another in the once upon a time in the space of eternal's past creating the most beautiful real life fairy tale that little prince and princes dream of until they are in the present.

My mind is overloaded with her beautiful face, I know it can only be GOD's grace to give me favor, to bless, and allow me to have one of HIS's best. He created you so elegantly and stylish as the scripture speaks on you, I know it to be true because I saw you in my dream and we were destined, on time, at this junction. Your energy has given me multiple doses of pure dopamine born before the first star of the universe that appeared in the first solar system of planets GOD created. It causes my heart to beat new life throughout my body to the very core of my DNA, never leaving the fresh scent of her love as pure as the awakening dew.

I'll love you infinity. Our love was created in

eternity past, brought to the present, to last in the future. You are my heartbeat in many worlds, and if the cosmos created a thousand more worlds, I would love you there infinity as though our love was still anew. She whispers gently in my ear, "my love, my energy is now yours, and your energy is now mine. It's the vibrations that play on my heart strings, it's the life force of my Godly soul that keeps me protected, it's my heavens of heavens. I whispered back to her, "you are the Universe that my Godly soul travels through to have peace, joy, and love. You are a fruit that I now have that will always fill the hunger of my passion. I have craved you since the beginning of my existence.

Ecstasy is her name...

~Poetic Storm (Christopher W. Strahan)

Phenomenal Lover

He sees her worth more than the diamonds created by
the Ancient of Days.

She knows he is full of confidence, she praises him
because of his Godly ways.

He loves the good and not harm she brings to him by
living an extraordinary life.

Knowing from the day they first met, she will always be
His favor, his loyal beautiful wife.

She's his peace, his comfort zone, she massages GOD's
temple, his body with her hands,

His love flows deep for her within the veins under his
finite skin, her wishes are his commands.

She feeds his hungry erotic energy that vibrates on a
frequency and every day they discover,

Why he moves to the beat of her heart playing a sweet
melody being her Phenomenal Lover.

She gets up before the sunrise preparing his garments
and nutrients for the day,

it inspires the birds to sing new songs as the trees wake
up back and forth, they sway.

He goes out working, providing the vision and desires
which gives GOD Glory,

He thinks of her and how she is like a sweet anointing
of oil as his mind writes a story.

His mind compares her above every wonder in the
world before there was space and time,

He's anxious to get back home and serenade her with
his words by action created through a rhyme.

He touches her in places that sends her body vibrating
and every day they discover,

Why he moves to the beat of her heart playing a sweet
melody being her Phenomenal Lover.

He rests his head upon her breast and gaze into her eyes
which are the windows of paradise,

They create new soul ties every second that are so
beautiful and clear like transparent ice.

She is his Rose of Sharon, his lily in every valley, his
sweetest passion fruit, ever so divine.

His loves leaps over mountains, bound over hills, and
moves through a tsunami's strongest line.

He says to her, "you are the good thing my soul loves,

because of you I'm blessed with many favors,

you are my ministry, my love for you, to the nostrils of
our Heavenly Father is a sweet flavor HE savors."

She feeds his hungry erotic energy that vibrates on a

frequency and every day they discover,

Why he moves to the beat of her heart playing a sweet
melody being her Phenomenal Lover.

~Poetic Storm (Christopher W. Strahan)

I Thought

I thought that I've seen beauty walk in my imagination
when I heard you sing the words of Amazing Grace.

I thought that I'd known love, but it was planted

in the deepest part of your heart for me when I gazed
upon your face.

I felt the love of your energy move my heart to the
sound on a frequency symptomatic beat.

It beats to your soul, and it danced to your tune

I couldn't stand from the excitement,

no longer on my feet.

You were the most beautiful songbird singing to my
heart, your voice is like melody when I hear you speak.

Every time I hear you utter my name through the
atmosphere we share together, suddenly, I get
weak.

I thought the rose I saw was fragrant, the vibrant color
of the grass was green, the sky seemed to be blue.

I thought nature was wonderful, in its awesome beauty,
but I saw better when I laid eyes on you.

I thought the sun was shining brightly through solar
systems.

I thought when I saw beauty in the second Heaven,

I had seen it all.

I thought that I was standing strong, but your illuminated radiant glow made me fall.

Fainted and landing on clouds created by love,

I knew that GOD made you from desires that came from rib, my thought process made a manifestation and out of the most wonderful part was your name.

~Poetic Storm (Christopher W. Strahan)

Can You Stand Rain?

In the Spring Time flowers bloom as the way my love
does for you. The grass grows tall in meadows,

sounds of winds harmonize in falsettos. Sweet cherries
aroma signifying scent, reminds me of the intimacy we
reinvent. Our energy procreates, when I say your name,
It's pouring outside.

Can you stand the rain?

Summer Time, Summer Time the sun shines so bright,
but nothing is greater than our days and nights.

We come together with each particle of our emotion,
giving a cool feeling of rendezvous breeze fresh off the
ocean.

As we look at the horizon, seeing the united colors

makes our hearts dance in sync like the wings of a
butterfly flutters.

The stars twinkle in the night sky, vibrations of our
energy so the same.

It's pouring outside. Can you stand the rain?

Autumn Time, the Earth gives off dew radiation to the
surface. GOD's eternal flow is working, bringing us
together for a purpose.

The trees of the leaves begin to fall to the ground,

I do the same and time stands still when you are around.

It's now harvest time, let me gather the fruit from your garden,

giving me thoughts from my imagination creating a margin Where you are manifested from my desires as

I call your name.

It's pouring outside. Can you stand the rain?

In the Winter it's cold, but you will keep me warm.

The greatest fire to me is to be in your arms. When it grows our love becomes an eternal flame. It forms a density that only our devotion claims.

You keep me warm during cold sleepless nights and in the cosmos our energy takes multiple flights. In the sleet or snow, I'll call out your name.

It's pouring outside. Can you stand the rain?

All the year around my love grows stronger.

I'll love you for always, for eternity, even longer.

I'll always be there through the good times and bad, just being near you is the best I ever had.

You walk into my thoughts when we are apart each day, I feel you like the four seasons embracing my existence in every way.

What do you think? Do you think this is a game?

I'll love you through tornadoes. Can you stand the Rain?

~Poetic Storm (Christopher W. Strahan)

My Enchanted Moment

I want to lie on the ground,

and stare into beauty beyond space, the stars twinkle
with a vibrancy.

into the enchanted image of your face.

I want to say the sound of your name

allowing it to vibrate off my tongue, rejuvenated
continuously through the night atmosphere now you're
unconscious and hallucinated.

I see you out of my imagination there now, looking
down from a fantasy at me,

with that enchanted seductive smile,

the true diamond within you I like to see.

When you shine, you make the universe glow.

If inspiration had another definition, it would be you.

Your vibrations continue to send me on a flight to the
very essence of time making me feel brand new.

When I heard you speak the and say, "close your eyes",
"tell me that I hold the other key to what you see",

I see only two people within our intimate circle, forever
where it was meant to be just you and me.

We're walking the shoreline waiting on me to hear, with
our feet getting wet listening to your beat, out a love you
never experienced but longed,

for before you existed as the sun gives of its radiant
heat.

~Poetic Storm (Christopher W. Strahan)

Power of The Word

Preaching the Word of GOD

Not only that but Praising the LORD. Now here's what I'm going to do,

listen close friend because I'm talking to you. Don't give into the Devil,

he's not even on GOD's level.

You might not understand what I'm saying, you see, you can defeat and beat the devil heat.

You can you use the WORD Haven't you heard,

the Devil is in a mess,

He won't be able to handle this,

so now you found a way to put the devil down to the ground,

but listen up to a little story,

straight out of the Bible from the LORD's category.

First, I was cooling the church house and relaxing with my Bible.

I didn't expect that we were going to have a revival. The music was jumping,

the praise and worship was bumping

the atmosphere was groovy, I had to do something. I put my Bible down and stood up to my feet, a double dose of the Holy Ghost made me give praise to the beat.

I heard the preacher come up from the pulpit and say, UMMMM HMMMM well welll...back into the Bible days When Yahshua healed people they were so amazed.

Of the HIS greatest works on planet Earth,

but that didn't stop Satan from doing his dirt.

Jesus gave us rules to live by from Heaven up high.

When a person that doesn't love you whose full of hate, love them anyway, that's right to date.

You see Jesus went around healing pain and sorrow, telling HIS disciples about tomorrow.

I'm Poetic Storm, by the blood I'm free.

Stepping black to give GOD the Glory in the place to be.

~Poetic Storm (Christopher W. Strahan)

Scriptures

Keys to a Stronger Marriage

Love is patient, love is kind. It does not envy, it does not boast, it is not proud. It does not dishonor others, it is not self-seeking, it is not easily angered, it keeps no record of wrongs.

~ 1 Corinthians 13:4-5

"Pastor was swinging on his porch as one of his deacons came over to talk with him. "Pastor, I've got something to tell you. I've never told this to a soul, it's extremely difficult to tell you this now, but my wife and I have had a fight almost every day for the past 30 years of our marriage."

The pastor was taken back. He looked away. He nervously took a sip of his coffee. He didn't know what to say. The young Pastor replied, "Everyday?" "Yes, just about every day." "Did you fight today before you came to church?" "Yes." "Well, how did it end up?" "She came crawling to me on her hands and knees." "MY Goodness what did she say?" "Come out from under that bed you coward and fight like a man!"

Love is patient and kind. Love is not jealous or boastful or proud or rude. It does not demand its own way. It is not irritable, and it keeps no record of being wronged.

Listen to 1 Corinthians 13:4-5 So, no matter what I say, what I believe, and what I do, I'm bankrupt without love. Love never gives up.

Love cares more for others than for self.

Marriage Therapy often calls for active listening, plus while affirming your spouse through paraphrasing, validation and positive feedback.

No interruptions, really listening while giving positive feedback such as- "So I hear you saying you want me to treat you as your best all time friend. I will do that, I can, yes, I will do that for you! "Can I tell you, "Many marital conflicts don't ever get resolved. There are always issues around: In- laws, children, and money Etc. Couple's that retain mutual respect and understanding…stay together. Your attitude plays out over the long haul."

Proverbs 12:18(NIV) The words of the reckless pierce like swords, but the tongue of the wise brings healing.

Listen up men and go ahead and swallow hard. One day three men were walking along and came upon a raging, violent river. They needed to get to the other side but had no idea of how to do it. The first man prayed to God saying, "Please God, give me the strength to cross this river." Poof! God gave him big arms and strong legs, and he was able to swim across the river in about two hours. Seeing this, the second man prayed to God saying, "Please God, give me the strength and ability to cross this river." Poof! God gave him a rowboat and he was able to row across the river in about three hours. The third man had seen how this worked out for the other two, so he also prayed to God saying, "Please God, give me the strength, ability, and intelligence to cross this river." And Poof! God turned him into a woman.

She looked at the map, then walked across the bridge.

Remember, Marriage is a special relationship created by

God. According to Matthew 19:6 You're no longer two, but one."

Keys when Conflicts Arise

Attack the problem, not each other.

Ephesians 5:21(NIV) Submit to one another out of reverence for Christ.

There's a real problem and sometimes the problem tries to divide- I say, "Attack it- pray over it!"

Again, attack the problem not each other. Most bad marriage problems stem from selfishness. "I want it my way!" When conflicts arise- You need to be heard, stay calm and your partner's more likely to take you seriously. For you to be taken seriously, you have to stay calm. This in return, allows the Lord to speak His peace and answer over the situation.

Paul wrote in Philippians 4:6-7(NIV) Do not be anxious about anything, but in every situation, by prayer and petition, with thanksgiving, present your requests to God. 7And the peace of God, which transcends all understanding, will guard your hearts and your minds in Christ Jesus.

Ephesians 4:32(NIV) Be kind and compassionate to one another, forgiving each other, just as in Christ God forgave you.

Kindness multiplying into becoming tenderhearted, forgiving one another- this all, breeds calmness. When conflicts arise- Choose the best time to address the issues, not when you're both tired and kids are hungry.

Remember, these are not suggestions. 1 Thessalonians 5:11(NIV) Therefore encourage one another and build each other up, just as in fact you are doing.

Song of Songs 4:9

Is it just me, or does this verse read like a K-C & JoJo Love Ballet? For real, I'll take Solomon's verses over the Drama filled «Empire» show any day! They're catchy enough to rival any modern Gospel R&B star, and they are just too sweet for words. My heart's all aflutter.

Don't worry about composing the perfect love note for your BAE (Before anyone else); this Bible verse about love speaks for itself. Leave it with a small, thoughtful gift and you're golden!

Things to ponder on...

Norman Vincent Peale and his book, "The Power of Positive Thinking." When he first wrote the book, he did not really like it and did not think it would amount to anything so he threw it in the garbage can. His wife saw it and sent it off to the publisher. It became his moniker. "Translated into fifteen languages and with more than 7 million copies sold in book and audio formats around the world, THE POWER OF POSITIVE THINKING is unparalleled in its extraordinary capacity for restoring the faltering faith of millions of people in themselves."

Most people, if not all, have the amazing gift of not seeing the potential in something they are doing. Our perspective on something is never perfect because it changes. Our perspective when we are 13 years old is quite different from when we are 21. And today, our perspective is quite different than it was 25 years ago.

Our perspective changes as we change and is affected by our personal experiences.

When we come to the groom as presented here in this fourth chapter, we get an insight into the bride through the eyes of the groom. This is a most remarkable picture.

Theme...

The basis of my fellowship and the fullness of my joy is to understand who you are in each other's eyes.

When you look at one another, what do you see? When you're truly in-love, and love one another on each level of love, then it's quite different from what the world sees. We are all obsessed with outward appearance that we fail to realize that it makes no impression whatsoever on our mate. We see not only the beautiful outside appearance, but also beyond the exterior and gaze upon the interior beauty of one another. When we allow God to be the foundation of our relationship, be assured that Christ penetrates deep into the soul that has been born again. When we become "alive in Christ," that interior aspect comes alive. It is that which draws the attention and affection of Christ.

Several aspects concerning the groom are brought to light in this passage. If we understand this, we will have a greater appreciation of our relationship and fellowship with God through the eyes of our marriage.

His Perception of the Bride.

First, we need to contrast his perception with our perception. If we do not understand this, we are not going to understand the basis of our relationship. Our perceptions are based upon our experiences, education and so forth. These things change with time. Everybody's perception would be different because everybody has different experiences. When two people look at one thing, they are looking at it from two different perceptions. What one sees the other does not see. That is because our perceptions are based upon time and therefore limited.

When we come to the groom, we need to see that this is completely different in that his perceptions do not change.

His perception is based upon who he is.

Malachi 3:6(NIV) – "I the Lord do not change. So, you, The descendants of Jacob, are not destroyed."

Hebrews 13:8(NIV) – "Jesus Christ the same yesterday, And today, and forever."

In other words, the groom is not confined to the time element that we are confined to. He does not change, He cannot change, there is no reason for him to change. I believe we can honestly say that his perception is based upon "perfect wisdom." The word "perfect" here indicates that there is nothing lacking in his wisdom and understanding. So, because this is true, he looks at the bride and sees the bride as she was created to be through the redeeming power of the blood of the Lord Jesus Christ. He sees her in her true glory. Nobody sees the bride quite like the groom.

His Pleasure in the Bride.

This aspect is greatly emphasized especially here in the passage before us. He sees the bride not as an object but rather as someone to fulfill his personal pleasure. I know we have taken this in the area of lust and depravity, but we need to understand this in light of the purity that is associated both with the groom and with the bride following her redemption. The aspect of this pleasure is that he appreciates who the bride really is. Not only that, but he delights in expressing that appreciation in many ways; blessings and favors. Everything the bride has the groom gave.

He talks about her "beauty." Nobody can see her beauty quite like the groom. The happiness of the groom expresses his appreciation of the bride's beauty. If we place this in context, we will see that both the bride and the groom are brought together in the fulfillment of true pleasure. Sometimes as Christians, we pooh-pooh the idea of pleasure. The reason for this is that pleasure has been twisted completely out of context and focused on the wrong perception. My opinion is that the aspects of "lust" are used by the devil to humiliate the groom. Unfortunately, all of mankind finds itself on the side of the devil in this regard.

If you look at all of creation, starting with the first chapter of Genesis, you will see that only man is created for God's pleasure. Upon the creation of everything it says, "God saw that it was good." The creation was not made typically for God's pleasure. When it comes to man here is what God says, "And God said, Let us make man in our image, after our likeness:" (Genesis 1:26).God said to Jeremiah, "Before I formed thee in the belly I knew thee; and before thou camest forth out of the womb I sanctified thee, and I ordained thee a prophet unto the nations" (Jeremiah 1:26).

Very simply put, when God looks at me, he sees his image, and nothing is more important as far as God is concerned. The block has been sin, but Jesus Christ died on the cross to break the power of sin in our life. What is the purpose of that? So, we can all go to heaven when we die? The purpose of that was so that God can look at us once again and see himself. God's greatest joy is in seeing his image reflected from our soul.

His Pursuit of the Bride.

The groom's perception of us and his pleasure in us fuels his pursuit of us. God is pursuing us.

Francis Thompson (1859-1907) emphasizes this in his poem "The Hound of Heaven."

Christ, as the hound of Heaven, pursues us with all the vigor of heaven. He is determined to find us in order to fellowship with us. Jesus says, "Ye have not chosen me, but I have chosen you, and ordained you, that ye should go and bring forth fruit, and that your fruit should remain: that whatsoever ye shall ask of the Father in my name, he may give it you" (John 15:16 KJV). This choice was a deliberate choice with a divine intention. He pursues us in order to have fellowship with us. Restore us to our rightful place in his heart. This pursuit is based upon his desire and not necessarily ours. Once he connects with us and reveals to us his affection for us, it creates within us a desire to know him. We pursue him because he first pursued us. The apostle Paul put it this way, "That I may know him, and the power of his resurrection, and the fellowship of his sufferings, being made conformable unto his death;" (Philippians 3:10 KJV). What we need to deal with are the many ways we make it hard for God to pursue us. We will see this throughout the book of Song of Solomon, especially the next section. Because of our imperfections, we make many mistakes. But the good news here is, because of his perfection our imperfections do not compromise his pursuit of us.

Conclusion...

The more we see the Lord the more we begin to understand who we are in Christ through one another in our relationship. If we focus on the exterior aspects of our life, we will end up in confusion and exhaustion. Many Christians are at this place. An obsession to keep up with the Joneses, and if we are going to escape this and have our lives rooted in our fellowship with Christ, we need to turn our back on the exterior elements of our life. We need to focus on that inner walk with God and keep Him in the center of our marriage. Each of us really need to celebrate each and every day with our spouses, our union and communion with God. To understand Christ is to understand the fellowship that I can have and that he desires me to have, to see ourselves how God wants us to see one another through His eyes.

Proverbs 17:9 Whoever would foster love covers over an offense, but whoever repeats the matter separates close friends.

This Bible verse about love doesn't quite read like a love note. However, it does hold a nugget of advice for aspiring couples. In context, this verse is one of many contrasting the upright and the wicked. Basically, it's a list of things "To Do" and "Not to Do' if you want to be a good person.

This verse encourages you to be discreet in your personal relationships.

Do you remember when your parents sat you down and taught you how to make friends?

Remember the 3-step process every child is given? Neither do I.

The truth is in the earliest years of our lives, we generally relate to whoever we have around us. It's not something many of us think about much. In our earliest years we just seemed to become friends with someone our parents had us play with, a neighbor or kids at school. What we find is that as we get older, it can actually get harder to find and form friendships. There are fewer groups we simply belong to, like in grade school. We can become more hesitant and guarded. We often don't know where to begin, and everybody is so busy. We don't even know how to try.

In our romantic culture we are suckers for the part of the story of how two people "find" each other sense of fate whether a best friend or romantic love. It is important to realize our relationships are found within the small sphere of our lives, 7 billion people, so any sense that what is being found is the "one" is a little misguided.

Anyone's spouse is their soulmate because they found a good compliment and FORMED a relationship.

Anyone's best friend is not the best because they went through 7 billion, but because they found a good connection and then allowed it to grow. We never just find a spouse or a friend. We find a good initial opportunity, but then the relationship forms over time. The process will be different for each of us because we have different circumstances and personalities. I want to encourage you to not waste time comparing your relational life to others.

In the time of Jesus, there were no apps for meeting people, but there was the local well that women drew water from, learning the exchange of trades at the mini market. Don't miss that he shared in our humanity.

When we look at Jesus what we see is a life of relationships, and when we look, we must not look in such a way that we can't imagine and see humanity. The Gospels focus almost exclusively on his years of ministry, emerging as the Messiah starting at the age of 30. We see the significant formation of relationships, so let's consider what we can learn about finding and forming relationships from his model and teaching and some of the wisdom of the Scriptures that he affirmed. If we look to Jesus what we discover is a picture of a relational life that can help us identify the different spheres that reflect something of a healthy way in which our lives experience connection. We all know that there are different levels of connection.

We have different circles around us that we share life in different ways.

The life of Jesus can help us see these. More importantly it can give us some perspective on how to better understand our own relationship to these spheres. I want to note that many choose different terms to associate with them, these are those I felt fit best. I chose not to use the word "friendship" for any one sphere because while we often do use the word friendship to speak of those uniquely close, we also can speak of many people as being our friends. Jesus himself was referred to as a "friend of sinners" because he attended meals with some lives, and he spoke of being friends to many. I suspect the words used to refer to friendships have long been used with different levels of closeness, and that is really the point of what we discover. We discover a world of broader connections that forms closer and deeper connections.

Jesus' first friend was his mother and no doubt also his father Joseph. His human existence depended on them. Joseph appears to have died at a relatively young age, and somewhere after Jesus has likely turned 13, deemed a young man in Jewish culture, and his ministry which

42

began at the age of 30. We can imagine several years of dependence on this woman as he grew. When Jesus takes on the world, and the cosmic claim over it, he doesn't emerge like the mysterious Clint Eastwood gunslinger, who rides into town, saves the day, and then rides back to his loner life. He comes to earth rooted in his human dependence where all formation of relationships begins.

When God came to show divine love amidst a wounded world, he didn't avoid such dependency, he embraced it as part of what love involves. We can see this as He sought the joys of friendship, companions to travel with, share meals with, and shared a life with during His earthly journey.

When faced with sorrow and fear he sought the comfort of his friends. He dared to rely on others, and some of his most painful times were the failures of those lives.

He depended on the provisions and companionship of others. I believe that embracing the care and provision of others was a part of his love for others. Jesus could embrace dependency because, when based on healthy needs, it was never understood as a weakness, or a flaw but as something beautiful.

In John 15, he says to the disciples, "Tonight I no longer call you servants. A servant does not know his master's business." See? Letting in. "But tonight, I call you friends. Now love one another as I love you. I am laying down my life for my friends." When Jesus Christ said that, suddenly the whole history of the world can be understood in terms of friendship. God was a friendship. The Christian God, the biblical God, is a friendship: Father, Son, Holy Spirit knowing and loving one another.

Therefore, he made us in his image, meaning we need friendship. You know, back in Genesis 3 when it talks about how God came walking in the cool of the garden to talk to Adam and Eve? Walking with someone is the Hebrew metaphor for friendship. To walk with someone, to walk together through life, is a metaphor for friendship. What that means is God made us for friendship, made us for friendship with him, made us for friendship with one another.

But we turned away from him. You know, when you betray a friend, what happens? Usually, the friend turns on you. This is what Jesus Christ is telling us he did. He says, "I am the ultimate friend. I am the ultimate friend who loves at all times. I am the one born for adversity. I am the ultimate friend who is going to cleave to you at infinite cost to myself so you will not be ruined. Here's how. I am the ultimate friend whose wounds are the wounds of love, because instead of inflicting them, I'm going to take them." The Bible says blessed are the wounds of a friend. How much more blessed are they when they are not inflicted but received?

Because Jesus Christ, on the cross, lost his friendship with God so we could have friendship with God. Jesus Christ, on the cross, experienced what we should have experienced so he could basically say, He was the perfect friend. He let you in. How much more of an emotional connection do you want? Look at his arms nailed open for you. How much more open do you want Him to be? There's the ultimate friend. He lets you in. Also, he never lets you down. Because in the garden of Gethsemane, as he saw his best friends falling asleep on him, denying him, betraying him, the Father comes and says, "You are going to have to go to hell, or you're going to lose your friends." Jesus said, "I'll go to hell."

There is a friend who sticks closer than a brother, so we're not ruined. There is a friend who goes to hell, so we're not ruined. If you know that, that liberates you to be the friend you need to be. If I know Jesus Christ has let me all the way in, He trusts me, and He loves me no matter what, then I can move out not being afraid of rejection.

Genesis 29:20(NIV)

So, Jacob served seven years to get Rachel, but they seemed like only a few days to him because of his love for her.

Bob Moeller writes: "I never met my grandmother. She died on the dusty, lonely plains when my father was 17 years old. Yet my father credits her with pointing him toward God. A few summers ago, when I attended a large family reunion, I heard some unknown history about my grandmother, now gone for over 50 years. She had been a mail-order bride. My grandfather was homesteading on the prairie where there were very few women. She had answered an advertisement he had placed in the paper. As my grandfather was dying, he asked everyone to leave the room except my two oldest sisters. He was then 89, a widower for nearly 30 years. `Do you know why I never remarried?' he asked in a raspy voice. They shook their heads no. "`Because when your grandmother died, I realized I could never love another woman as much as I loved her.' And then writes, "If my grandfather and grandmother began their marriage through a mail-order arrangement and yet learned to love each other that deeply, who's to say that God can't do something just as extraordinary in your marriage? If, like Jacob and Leah, you started out all wrong, who's to say God can't use your relationship to bless not only your lives but future generations as well?"

Our Scripture is the story of Jacob, whose name means "the one who takes the rightful place of another." Jacob was a weasel and a deceiver, having conspired with his mother to trick his own father into giving him the family blessing and inheritance rather than to his older brother, Esau. When Esau found out, he sought to kill Jacob forcing his mother to send Jacob away to her relatives to save his life. When Jacob arrived at the well where his mother's family waters their flocks and a shepherdess named Rachel was there. It was love at first sight. When he met her, he kissed her and began to weep what appeared to be tears of joy. He negotiates with her father Laban for her hand in marriage, agreeing to work for 7 years to wed her. When the wedding day finally came, Laban arranges the party. When it was time for Jacob and Rachel to consummate the relationship, unbeknownst to him his new father-in-law gives him Leah who is described as weak-eyed or very unattractive, rather than Rachel who was beautiful. In that culture, a woman would have been heavily veiled, so Jacob was none the wiser. They consummated the marriage in the dark of the night and Jacob rolls over in the morning and the woman beside him is not the woman of his dreams.

The same thing has happened to many couples. We wake up one day and think we've married the wrong person.

Three things contribute to this. First are our differences. Bill Hybels writes, "I dated Lynne (his wife) off and on for five years, but it was not until after the wedding date that I found out the awful truth. Lynne was strange. She was not normal like me." She turned out to be a near recluse and Bill was an off the charts extrovert. She was oversensitive.

She'd watch a sad movie and couldn't sleep because she was up crying all night. Bill would tell her about a couple who had gotten in financial debt, and she couldn't believe that he wasn't going to help them. His way was to let them dig themselves out and learn their lesson the hard way. Lynne had to have everything planned even on vacations and Bill loved to live by spur of the moment. He then goes on to tell the story of Pygmalian, who found a unique way to solve the differences between him and his potential wife. Out of the finest ivory, he sculpted the woman of his dreams.

When done, he bowed and prayed, and she came to life, and they lived happily ever after. That's what many of us try to do with our spouses. We take a chisel and chip away all the rough edges, flaws and differences of our spouses and try to make them to be more like us. We each think we're normal and thus try to change our spouses. If there is one thing, I've learned in 25 years of marriage it's this: God has this way of putting people together who are totally different. If you are a spender, I can guarantee you married a saver. One of you is a neat freak and the other is freakishly messy. John Gray's bestseller says, "Men are from Mars and Women are from Venus." I'm starting to think we're living in completely different galaxies. Here's the moral of the story: no one is wrong here. It's just a matter of perspective. Just because you're different and that may bring conflict doesn't mean that you've married the wrong person. It just means that you're human and the adage "opposites attract" is true.

Second is unmet expectations. Jacob had an expectation that he's marrying the beautiful Rachel, but he wakes up with her older sister Leah. We all go into marriage with expectations. Expectations come from many sources such as parents, values, our culture or even Hollywood.

There are three very common expectations for marriage. Couples expect their marriage to work out and never end in divorce, to be faithful to each other in every way and that their marriage will be a smooth ride without any major upheavals or adjustments. Expectations can be even smaller than that. He has an expectation of what she's going to wear to bed. She has an expectation that he's going to love her no matter what she wears and that he just wants her to be comfortable. The problem is that most of the time our expectations aren't vocalized, it's just assumed the other person views it the same way. And that's when we become disenchanted, disappointed, upset, angry, bitter, and sometimes even taking the attitude that we'll never make it. Expectations are the causes of most conflict in marriages.

Third, underestimating God's blessing. When Jacob is going to die, he must decide – to be buried with Rachel or Leah. Here's what he decides: "Then Jacob instructed them, 'Soon I will die and join my ancestors. Bury me with my father and grandfather in the cave in the field of Ephron the Hittite…. And there I buried Leah.'" Genesis 49:29-31, Jacob spent his whole life wanting someone else instead of the wife he had, and it created nothing but problems in his life. At the end of his life, the one who he thought was the wrong person was actually the one who had been the blessing. Don't make this mistake! Your spouse is a blessing to you, but we often forget that.

If you've been thinking that you're married to the wrong person, what are you to do? The relationship you're dreaming of isn't with someone else. You can have what you're looking for with the one you're with. But it's going to take 6 things. First, change how you see your spouse.

Your spouse is a child of God. They are special, unique, and made in God's image. Recognize that the one you're with is God's blessing to you.

Second, learn to fight fair. How? James 1:19-20 "So then, my beloved brethren, let every man be swift to hear, slow to speak, slow to wrath; for the wrath of man does not produce the righteousness of God." The question isn't if you fight in your marriage. The question is how well do you fight? One of the best things you can do is to create a set of ground rules for arguing, about what's warranted and what's not. Things like, "Under no circumstances will either of us raise our voice." No bringing up the past. No cuss words or name calling. So often when we fight, we want to win the battle. If you do, then you may lose the war. If only one of you wins, you both have lost because you're both on the same team. You must remember that you aren't enemies. Instead, your goal should be to find a common, agreeable solution for the good of your marriage, that builds trust in your relationship. No marriage has zero conflict - the married people who don't fight are being honest and real with each other. It's about fighting well.

Third, confront issues you've been avoiding. Many husbands and wives never confront the issues they have. They stay silent allowing resentment to build up or they leave, taking the easy way out. You've got to deal with your issues. That's key to developing emotional intimacy. Fourth, is patience. Realize that change doesn't happen overnight. Once you confront the problems, it takes time to see the results.

You may even need to receive counseling to help you work through your problems. Fifth, is forgiveness because you can't make it work and still hold onto all the hurt. We're called to forgive as we have been forgiven. You can't live in the past and expect to have a future. Sixth, resolve to do whatever it takes. If you don't, it's not going to work. The relationship you want is possible with the person you're with as long as both of you are willing to put each other first and work at it. You can run from the problems you have in your relationship all in the name of "We're not soul mates" or you can have the courage to stay. Finding someone else won't solve it. The divorce rate of 2nd and 3rd marriages is more than 70%. One way to do that is to become the person God intends you to be. You didn't marry the wrong person. We just must be open to God transforming us into His image because that's the purpose of marriage, to shape and mold us in Christ's image. We can focus on our spouse being the wrong person, but maybe we need to focus on becoming the right person for our spouse.

One of the biggest challenges to marriage is marital drift. What happens to couples when they fall in love is they're intimately close, then they get married, kids come along with their extracurricular activities, and they focus so much of their time and energy on them. Careers take off and individual interests are developed and before you know it, you stop focusing on each other. One day, you then look at each other and say, "Who are you?" Then you start to think that maybe you've married the wrong person and that you need a new start rather than getting real in these relationships and dealing with your issues. The day we let go of the idea that there's this soul mate out there for us and looking to the next one as our ticket to happiness, we'll start trying to fix the marriage we're in. The truth is that great marriages choose to make it work. Love is a choice!

Not Good to be Alone

Genesis 2:18-24

The Lord God said, "It is not good for the man to be alone. I will make a helper suitable for him."

Now the Lord God had formed out of the ground all the wild animals and all the birds in the sky. He brought them to the man to see what he would name them; and whatever the man called each living creature, that was its name. 20 So the man gave names to all the livestock, the birds in the sky and all the wild animals.

But for Adam[a]no suitable helper was found. 21 So the Lord God caused the man to fall into a deep sleep; and while he was sleeping, he took one of the man's ribs[b] and then closed up the place with flesh. 22 Then the Lord God made a woman from the rib[c]he had taken out of the man, and he brought her to the man.

The man said,

"This is now bone of my bones

and flesh of my flesh;

she shall be called 'woman,'

for she was taken out of man."

That is why a man leaves his father and mother and is

united to his wife, and they become one flesh.

Man is not just another animal. Both physically, and morally, 'Man was made upright' After all, man was made in the image of God. God 'breathed into his nostrils the breath of life'.

Man was first made a single male but is immediately afterwards referred to as a plurality much as God refers to Himself as a plurality. Man was created with an inbuilt need for company, community, and fellowship.

Our passage takes us back to a time before the 'all very good' of Genesis 1:31. It speaks of a time when it was not (yet) all good. Created in the image of God, man craves such companionship as exists within the Trinity. Even those who are called to the single life need the security of community.

Before it is 'all very good,' one thing must be resolved: "It is not good for man to be alone". The LORD would make a help meet for man, literally a "helper like opposite him." Man needed a helper, one like himself but different, opposite, complementary, to stand upright beside him.

Man was given dominion over all other species upon earth. Man was blessed with intelligence and given authority and ability to name the animals. But he was not going to find his helper here.

Now, the fact that woman was to be created "for" man does not in any sense mean that she was to be subjugated and enslaved by him. Rather, the woman was created 'because of the man' because of his lack, because of his need of a helper.

The word "helper" does not suggest domination, but partnership. The word "helper" does not suggest subservience, but a certain strength and reliability. Interestingly, the word "helper" is used in the Bible more often of God than of anyone else. It is interesting to see God's method in making and creating woman. First, we see that it was entirely the work of God: the man was passive throughout. If this was a surgical procedure, then God was the surgeon. Man was asleep.

Second, the woman was created out of the man's side. God took the "rib" and "built" the woman. Then, as the Father of the bride, the LORD God presented her to the man.

Adam's reaction bordered on the ecstatic. Perhaps we may regard this as the first ever love song: "This is now bone of my bones, and flesh of my flesh". It is at least poetic.

In modern idiom, Adam was acknowledging that here at last was his own flesh and blood. Here at last, was "Woman" to stand upright beside "Man."

The man calling his new partner in life "Woman, because she was taken out of Man" was not an exercise of dominion as it had been in the naming of the animals, but an expression of joy at what God had accomplished!

The ordinance of marriage was instituted. Marriage is of a man and a woman, each leaving their parents to cleave to one another, and to become "one flesh." All was well in the Garden, at least for the time being.

Whatever their respective responsibilities in relation to the fall of mankind, as related in Genesis 3, we can be sure that God already had it covered. The provision was there in the judgment against the serpent, which included a promise pointing directly to Jesus, as THE seed of the woman.

Death was introduced into the world as a consequence of sin; but in faith, Adam now 'called his wife's name Eve, because she was the mother of all living'. Meanwhile, God in His grace provided skins (requiring the sacrifice of animals) to cover man's sin.

Finally, 'In the fullness of time, God sent forth His Son, born of a woman… that we might receive the adoption as sons'.

Dating Tips for Believers

Main Scripture: Genesis 2:18

Ahhh, Dating. Dating makes everybody feel like a dummy at some point or another. You see that girl or guy of your dreams, and you instantly get sweaty palms (or pits), your face turns red, and you have those butterflies in your stomach. You often may not know what to say, or you try and put your best foot forward, and then you say something totally stupid. It's especially difficult if you're meeting someone for the first time. Adam and Eve had the first ever blind date! I bet the first thing he said was "WO, MAN!" And thus, she was named, woman. After that, he probably didn't know what to say, but since they were both naked, he didn't really have to think of something to say so she'd take her shirt off.

Things have changed quite a bit since then, and over the years, dating has transformed into this who's who, popularity contest among classmates, friends, co-workers, and celebrities. All of them vying to find and date the right person, and some of them not wanting to get caught, while others flaunt their newly found soul mate like it's the latest PRADA bag. As if to say, "ooh, look what I've got. Isn't it HOT?!"

I guess I wonder sometimes, what is dating like for the average teenager or even now the average adult? What's the whole point of dating? What are some of your thoughts— what is the point of dating?

I had some of those same thoughts when I was a teenager. I used to think that you had to be dating someone to be cool. That's why I got a girlfriend—yeah, I wanted to make out with her, too. But, in reality, I wanted to be considered cool. About 25 years ago, I picked up this little book (and I do mean little) because I was having a little trouble finding and dating the right kind of woman. I thought it might have tips and tricks to help me in my pursuits.

I guess some of you guys right now would be asking yourself questions before asking a lady out on a date. What kind of skills should you try to acquire before you ask the woman of your dreams out? Is she going to say no if you don't know how to two step to that latest Billboard jam?

So, if you're ready, I'm going to give you some free advice—my own little dating for dummies that I've found from learning things the hard way, from reading a few dating books, and looking into what God's plan is for couples.

Dating is NOT just a game we play to have fun. Dating is fun, and meant to be enjoyable, but if you're not dating for some of the right reasons, then pain is in your future. Can you date and avoid pain? Probably not. I believe the main purpose for dating is to find the kind of person you want to marry, or to figure out who you are equally yoked for, and who will compliment you to enhance one another's lives.

Here's what we do know about God's plan: God designed man and woman at the beginning of time to be together, to procreate, and to fulfill each other's needs and desires. He also designed you to have a companion. Genesis 2:18 says, "and God said, 'it is not good for man to be alone; I will make a companion who will help him.'" So, God doesn't want you to be alone. If we know that God is the intelligent designer of this universe and he created you and me, and He doesn't want us to be alone, then it's only right to think that he's got some ideas about how to NOT be alone.

A problem that most people start off with in dating is just that. They try to do dating, and find the right person based on looks, and personality, and hobbies, and likes and dislikes, but they do all that without considering what God thinks, or what God has to say. If you're doing that, you're doing it all WRONG!!!

Dating for Believers # 1:

Start with an Intelligent Designer. Think about this for a minute. For many of you, there are special events coming up soon. Well, let's say I was put in charge of making your dress ladies. I know, it probably wouldn't even cross your mind to have me make it, but bear with me. You come to me, and you have these amazing drawings or pictures of your ideal dress for this special event, but what I end up creating after gathering my duct tape and frizzy material might look like something from the caveman era. However, if you take that idea for a dress to someone like Dolce and Gabbana, Ann Lowe, Yeezy and Fenty or some incredibly talented designer, then you're going to have the best-looking dress in the place. It's kind of like this, when you decide, you are ready to start dating, you automatically think you know how to find a good mate, and you start dating all these losers and you get your heart broken time after time, because you didn't take your ideas to the right designer. If God has your best interests in mind, which HE does, then you've got to include Him in the dating process.

Ecclesiastes 4:9-12, says, "9 Two people are better off

than one, for they can help each other succeed. 10 If one person falls, the other can reach out and help. But someone who falls alone is in real trouble. 11 Likewise, two people lying close together can keep each other warm. But how can one be warm alone? 12 A person standing alone can be attacked and defeated, but two can stand back-to-back and conquer. Three are even better, for a triple-braided cord is not easily broken."

God knows it's better to have two than one, but ultimately three is better than two! Solomon uses the illustration here of a triple-braided cord. Rope is used for a lot of stuff— tying things together, playing tug-of-war, and lots of other things, but the most useful thing a rope is used for is probably climbing. If I'm climbing up the side of a mountain, and I lose my grip, and the only thing between me and the ground is a rope, then I want that thing to be incredibly strong. If that rope only has two strands, it's weaker than one that has three strands. God says he wants to be that third strand in the cord, or the rope. He wants to be the part that ties your relationship together. It doesn't amaze me that 50% of marriages end in divorce if people that are dating don't start with an intelligent designer. Relationships that aren't designed and founded on God's principles are destined to fail.

Dating for Believers Tip #2: Make a LIST with your Designer.

When I decided to get serious about dating for the right reasons—which some of us haven't learned yet, I was just getting serious with my believer's walk with God. Usually, I just went to church because it was a great way to meet ladies, but I didn't figure on meeting this particular woman. I can't remember her name, but I remember one thing I learned from her. When we met, I looked at her Bible, and on the inside of the cover was taped a piece of paper. It was a list, and on that list were her requirements for a husband. It was a list of all the things she was looking for in a guy. After I talked to her for a while, it made me think.

If I had a list up to that point, it'd only have one thing on it... MUST BE GORGEOUS!!! I probably didn't even care if the women I hooked up with were even that HOTT. I decided that day to change my dating tactics. I sat down and made my own list. The Bible I had was about 20 years old---and I made my list and taped it to the inside. These were my requirements for a wife.

I continued to date a lot of women, and it seemed like none of them added up to the list. I was friends with a lot of women, but they never had it all. For me, the list was a steppingstone. I began to imagine how the woman I would marry would be. Ephesians 3:20(NLT) says, "Now glory be to God! By his mighty power at work within us, he is able to accomplish infinitely more than we would ever dare to ask or hope." God can do more than you or I can even imagine.

If you can think it, then God can beat it! So, when you're ready to get serious, make your list, and then be prepared to be amazed.

Dating for Believers Tip # 3: Shift your Focus.

A wise man once said, "if you aim for nothing, you'll hit it every time." I know if you've got God as your designer, and you've made your list, then you're ready to shift your focus. When we think about dating, we often always think of who might be good for us. Almost like shopping for a new car—what will this thing do for me to make me look better? I want to challenge you to shift your focus. Have you ever thought that if you are looking for a shiny new car, that if you look at yourself, you might actually be more like a beat-up jalopy of a ride. If you shift your focus, then you're probably realizing that you need a bit of work. When you take a look at your list, is it everything you're not? Do you even measure up?!?! Maybe it's time for you to Focus on yourself. Guys, are you a slob when you eat? Do you make rude jokes around women? Are you only after one thing? Do you only shower when you notice your dog or cat smells better than you? Ladies, do you only talk to guys who have nice cars? Does the idea of dating a geek repulse you? Are you afraid to get your hands dirty?

Some of these things might not keep you from getting the person of your dreams, but usually you attract what you are because energy goes where attention flows. When you know there are some things about you that aren't right, then you've got to get yourself a little makeover. Maybe it's your attitude, or the way you treat people. Maybe it's the things you do on a Friday night, or you've got to clean up that reputation of yours. Whatever it is, then shift your focus, and get to work.

This little book that I picked up about 10 years ago, hoping it would hold the key to all my dating nightmares and mistakes. They had made other "for dummies" books that seemed to have all the right answers to all my questions, so I thought I'd give it a shot. What I found in that little book might have worked for some practical purposes—what to wear on a date, where to meet people, how to ask someone out, among other things. One of the best things I learned from this book was that I had to get rid of my pickup lines! I would use some of the cheesiest lines to get women. I would actually spend time on the internet looking for good lines to tell women—some of you are thinking to yourself, "man, I'm that guy."

"Hey, can I have a quarter?" she'd say, "why?". "Because my mom told me to call home when I found the woman of my dreams."

"Did it hurt? —When you fell from heaven?"

"If I could rearrange the alphabet, I'd put U and I together."

If you're wondering whether or not these lines work, or if you're using your notes sheet to write these down---then you're definitely reading the right book, because Dating for Dummies is for YOU!

After I learned from this little book that using pick up lines is never a good idea, things for me started to turn around. Some of you want to date because you're looking for someone to be with, some of you want to date because you're bored sitting at home, some of you want to date because all of your friends are dating. If any of you end up with a doll for a girlfriend, I'm sure we'll accept you, but that'd be a little weird!

People date other people because they want to feel good about themselves, they want to be accepted. Everybody wants to be loved. Right? Nobody really likes to be lonely. Is dating the only way to fulfill these needs?

I believe there's another way for Believers to think about dating. Around the time I picked up that little book "Dating for Dummies," I had heard of another book, "I Kissed Dating Goodbye." This one, I was sure wouldn't have any answers about how to get a date, but as I began to get serious about my relationship with God, I read it, and this book, is one that changed my life. I learned so much about myself, and God, and my ideas on dating.

After reading the book I didn't completely decide to kiss dating goodbye, but I had realized that not dating wasn't the point. The point was that I was going about the pursuit all wrong up to that point. I just wanted to date the best-looking women to be popular or look better in front of my friends...I didn't really care what God wanted for me.

I'm not going to pretend that we can cover all there is to know about God's desires for your dating life in two little weeks, but I want to cover the important stuff.

Dating for Believers Tip # 4: Don't Pursue STUPID love.

When people are asked about love, here is what they say: When someone loves you, the way they say your name is different. You know that your name is safe in their mouth.

Love is when a woman puts on perfume and a man puts on shaving cologne and they go out and smell each other.

Love is when you go out to eat and give somebody most of your food without making them give you any of theirs.

Love is when your puppy licks your face even after you left him alone all day.

I know my older sister loves me because she gives me all her old clothes and has to go out and buy new ones.

When you love somebody, your eyelashes go up and down and little stars come out of you. It's easy to think that you're in love when you measure love by the feelings that you get. But love is more than feelings.

Philippians 1:9-10 says, "This is my prayer: that your love may abound more and more in knowledge and depth of insight, so that you may be able to discern what is best and may be pure and blameless for the day of Christ."

Paul is talking about smart love here, and not the kind of love that you think you know. You may think you're in love when you can't think of anyone else, or when you spend hours talking on the phone at night, or when your heart jumps when you see that person...but Paul is talking about a different kind of love. He says that smart love is knowing what is best, that smart love helps keep you pure in God's sight. The message says it like this: "Learn to love appropriately. You need to use your head and test your feelings so that your love is sincere and intelligent, not sentimental gush."

See, people do STUPID things, especially when they think they're in love. Does love motivate the guy who sleeps with his girlfriend when it's going to scar her emotionally and physically? Does love motivate the woman who leads a man on and breaks up with him after she finds someone better? NO! They both are motivated by selfish ambition. God wants you to pursue the kind of love that helps you know what is best. The kind of love that will keep you pure.

Dating for Believers Tip # 5: What's BEST might not be Popular.

You can be sure that deciding to do what's best in your dating life will NOT be popular in the world today, especially with social media, video broadcasting apps, and dating sites where folks will do and say whatever it takes to be popular. The choice you make will do just the opposite. I'm going to be brutally honest with you, YOU ARE NOT READY TO DATE, and have no business asking for someone's heart and affections if you can't back that up with a lifelong commitment.

Anna's wedding day was finally here. She planned for months and months, and in the small church with her family and friends, she was ready to take the vows with her fiancé, David. He gently took her hand, and they turned toward the altar. As the minister began to lead David and Anna through their vows, the unthinkable happened. A girl stood up in the middle of the congregation, walked quietly to the altar and took David's other hand. Another girl approached and stood next to the first, followed by another, and another. Soon there was a chain of six girls standing next to David. Anna felt her lip quivering as tears welled up in her eyes, "is this some kind of joke?" she whispered to David. "I'm sorry, Anna," he said, staring at the floor. "Who are these girls, David? What's going on?" she gasped. "They're girls from my past. Anna, they don't mean anything to me now, but I've given part of my heart to each of them." "I thought your heart was mine," she said. "It is. It is. Everything that's left is yours." A tear rolled down Anna's cheek, and then she woke up. When Anna woke up, she felt betrayed.

Then, she wondered how many men would be standing at the altar next to her.

Proverbs 4:23 says to guard your heart, for it is the wellspring of life. When you are choosing to date, you choose to give your heart and affections to each person you're with. I don't think that's smart love, and it's definitely not in your best interest to give away little pieces of yourself here and there and have little to offer that person that God has prepared for you.

Let me tell you what I think could be best in **Dating for Believers Tip #6: Choose to focus on friendships rather than dating.**

Dating tends to isolate people from their friendships.

When you start dating someone, not only do you give them part of your heart when you aren't ready, but you give them ALL your spare time. Your friendships suffer because of your new relationship. Then, six months later, your friends wonder where you've been. Why make that sacrifice? When you focus on friendships, even with the opposite sex, you get to learn all about them, without the mess of romance getting in the way.

If you're ready to get serious about this dating thing, then you have to ask yourself a serious question—To date or not to date?

When I decided to make that dating list, I knew that I'd probably never find someone that measured up if I continued to treat women the way I did. I had to ask God for a makeover myself. While I gave you a few dating tips for Believers, you may be looking at this last one and realizing it's never going to work for you without some help. I want to pray for you that you'd be able to let God in on your relationships. If that's you, that's been doing this dating thing all wrong without God's help and you want him to be your designer. If you know you need a makeover—whether it's extreme or not, and you're figuring out only God can help, then say this prayer.

Friends, Jesus (Yeshua) did come to save us from ourselves. All the rotten and no good things we do or have done can be wiped clean if we just ask Jesus to make it right. We like to say if you believe Jesus (Yeshua) died for you, admit you've messed up, surrender your life to God, and enter into a life of living for him, then you can be made over. If you're wanting that type of makeover, then now's the time.

Prayer

Our Father in heaven, so much in the dating scene today seems so broken — unnecessary ambiguity, unhealthy communication, fear of commitment, boundaries crossed, and messy breakups. Because I'm yours, I desperately want my dating to be different. Set my relationship apart from every fallen example around me. Allow my love and respect for others to say something profound and beautiful about your Son, even when I make mistakes or sin against my significant other. Forgive me right now for everything that has caused me to miss your will for my life. Renew my spirit, and give me a fresh anointing, and discernment to know the one that is equally yoked for me according to the desires you have given to my heart. The line between affection and infatuation can blur quickly in a relationship, blinding us to you and to ourselves. Having "fallen in love," we lose touch with our fallenness. Satan steps into the euphoria and deceives us into ignoring, overlooking, or excusing sin.

We compromise in relationships in ways we never would otherwise. God, blow away the fog of any infatuation, and fill our eyes with your truth and beauty. When every fiber of every muscle in our bodies wants to give into temptation, ignite our hearts to reject sin's filthy promises and to prefer you and your righteousness. Father, guard us from isolating ourselves and our relationship from other believers. The more time we spend one-on-one with each other, the less time we spend with other important people in our lives. That distance is one of the greatest dangers in dating. Draw the men and women we need into our feelings, our communication, and our decision-making. Bring us other Believers who love us enough to ask hard questions. When the temptation will be to date off in a corner, weave our relationship into real, consistent, and engaged community. We feel how vulnerable we are in dating — the uncertainty, the fragility, the volatility. It is not a safe love yet, because it is not yet sealed with our promises. If we are to truly, deeply, exclusively, freely, and passionately love each other, it must be as husband and wife. It must be inside the beautiful and mysterious oneness of marriage. So, give us clarity, God. We are waiting for you to make clear whether we should marry. We don't want to date one day longer than you would have us. We're pleading for wisdom in dating because we know how much you love to give it to those who ask. Above all, forbid that any love would begin to overshadow or replace our love for you. If either of us consistently draws us away from you, give us enough faith and love to walk away. Guard us from anyone who wants your place in our heart and lead us to a husband or wife who has already given all of their heart, soul, mind, and strength to you. Whether we ever marry or not, we pledge our love first and forever to you — from this day forward, for better, for worse, for richer, for poorer, in sickness and health — until death once and for all marries us to you. In Jesus (Yeshua) name I pray. Amen

Celebrating
Milestones

Whether you are in the first days of marriage or have already experienced a rich life together, it is important to celebrate milestones. Each year is linked with a gift idea. Below I will provide examples for anniversary gifts by year and briefly explain why each object represents the passage of varying amounts of time.

Traditional gifts became a symbolic metaphor to mark the years. As time passed, the gifts associated with each anniversary evolved alongside society. Modern gift ideas reflect items that have become more popular for couples today.

Some of them offer practical alternatives to luxury items.

Year	Traditional	Modern
1	Paper	Clock
2	Cotton	China
3	Leather	Crystal/Glass
4	Fruit/Flowers	Appliances
5	Wood	Silverware
6	Candy/Iron	Wood
7	Copper	Desk Set
8	Bronze	Linens/Lace
9	Pottery	Leather
10	Tin/Aluminum	Diamond Jewelry
11	Steel	Fashion Jewelry
12	Silk/Linen	Pearls

13	Lace	Textile/Furs
14	Animal/Animal Items	Gold Jewelry
15	Crystals	Watches
20	China	Platinum
25	Silver	Silver
30	Pearl	Pearl
35	Coral	Coral
40	Ruby	Ruby
45	Sapphire	Sapphire
50	Gold	Gold
60	Diamond	Diamond

The **First Year** of marriage is still considered to be a clean slate and a new beginning. Paper symbolizes the ability to write your own story.

~Traditional~

Gifts for Her
A signed book, a love note, monogrammed stationery

~Modern~

Gifts for Him
Tickets to a concert or sporting event

Your marriage has just begun! A clock represents the eternal amount of time you have together.

Second Year

~Traditional~

Cotton, slightly more durable than paper, shows the couple's lives becoming more intertwined.

Gifts for Her
A wristwatch

Gifts for Him
A small clock for his desk

~Modern~

Gifts for Her
A fine China vase, a vintage perfume bottle

Gifts for Him
An engraved mug

Gifts for Her
A bathrobe, a cotton throw pillow

Gifts for Him
Monogrammed towel, a sweatshirt from his alma mater

Third Year

~Traditional~

Leather covers and protects from the elements, much as a marriage should offer security.

Gifts for Her

A handbag, leather boots, a leather-bound notebook

Gifts for Him

A leather belt, a wallet

~Modern~

Glass is a reminder of the fragility of love and the care it requires.

Gifts for Her

Crystal jewelry, crystal candle holders

Gifts for Him

A pair of sunglasses, personalized wine glasses

Fourth Year

~Traditional~

After four years, the relationship begins to blossom and ripen! Fruit or flowers represent the state of bliss after four years together.

Gifts for Her

Rose or fruit-scented perfume, an edible bouquet

Gifts for Him

Tickets to the Rose Bowl, an Apple iPad

~Modern~

Appliances have become popular gifts for decorating your new home together. With so much new technology, you can also opt for a fun gadget!

Gifts for Her

An espresso machine, a GoPro camera

Gifts for Him

An Apple iPad, portable speakers

Fifth Year

~Traditional~

Roots and strength are now established. Strength and wisdom will continue to grow and flourish just like a tree continues to grow.

Gifts for Her

A wooden serving tray (with breakfast in bed), a wooden vase

Gifts for Him

A wooden rocking chair

~Modern~

New silverware is a sensible gift idea as the original wedding set is likely to be worn or tarnished after five years of use.

Gifts for Her

A new set of silverware

Gifts for Him

An engraved flask

Sixth Year

~Traditional~

Candy is sweet and serves as a reminder to keep the romance alive. Iron symbolizes the strength of a marriage that is now well-established.

Gifts for Her

Decadent truffles, a candy bouquet, an iron jewelry holder

Gifts for Him

Customized candies, golf clubs

~Modern~

Wood is strong, long-lasting, and continuously growing, much like a marriage.

Gifts for Her

A customized cutting board, a wooden framed photo

Gifts for Him

Barrel-aged whiskey, a wooden wall hanging

Seventh Year

~Traditional~

Cooper is a great conductor of heat which represents warmth, comfort, and safety, all part of a strong foundation.

Gifts for Her

Artisan copper jewelry, fine art with copper detailing

Gifts for Him

Mule mugs, a copper desk set

~Modern~

Another practical gift, a desk set, is often combined with something useful for the office like pens or a desk organizer.

Gifts for Her

Engraved letterhead, a desk organizer

Gifts for Him

A copper desk set, an engraved fountain pen

Eight Year

~Traditional~

Bronze is a blend of copper and tin and symbolizes the union of two lives.

Gifts for Her

A bronze vase, a bronze necklace

Gifts for Him

A bronze bottle opener

~Modern~

Linens serve as another replacement for old wedding gifts, like a nice set of sheets for your home. Alternatively, many opt for lace items like a new lace dress to make your wife feel beautiful.

Gifts for Her

A lace dress, fresh bed linens

Gifts for Him

A linen tie

Ninth Year

~Traditional~

Pottery is carefully molded from clay to create a piece of art, much as a marriage is shaped by experiences to create a life together.

Gifts for Her

A vase full of flowers, a customized coffee mug

Gifts for Him

A clay desk sculpture

~Modern~

Leather, on the other hand is durable, strong, and flexible, signifying the stability of a relationship.

Gifts for Her

A monogrammed leather wallet

Gifts for Him

A leather-banded watch

Tenth Year

~Traditional~

Tin was once used to protect iron from rust and corrosion. After 10 years together, a couple has proven their ability to protect each other and fight life's battles together.

Gifts for Her

New cookware

Gifts for Him

Grilling tools, a tin of his favorite treats

~Modern~

Diamonds reflect beauty and symbolize how precious a relationship is.

Gifts for Her

Simple diamond bracelet, diamond earrings

Gifts for Him

Diamond studded cuff-links

Eleventh Year

~Traditional~

Steel is a super strong substance, marking the durability of a relationship after 11 years together.

Gifts for Her

Stainless steel pots and pans, steel bottle opener

Gifts for Him

A Swiss army knife, steel cigar holder

~Modern~

Fashionable jewelry, on the other hand, is a way to flash your affection with a trendy item.

Gifts for Her

A trendy necklace

Gifts for Him

A fitness tracking bracelet

Twelfth Year

~Traditional~

Many difficulties have been faced together after 12 years. Now it's time for some smooth sailing and enjoying the finer things in life.

Gifts for Her

A silk slip, matching monogrammed silk robes

Gifts for Him

A silk tie, silk boxers, matching monogrammed silk robe

~Modern~

A pearl is a rare treasure which symbolizes the value of your relationship and the 12 years you've spent together.

Gifts for Her

A pearl necklace

Gifts for Him

Dinner at an oyster bar

Thirteenth Year

~Traditional~

Lace is both beautiful and elegant and symbolizes the perfection of a long-lasting relationship.

Gifts for Her

A lace shawl, a lace dress

Gifts for Him

New tennis shoes with bright laces

~Modern~

If you opt for the modern 13th anniversary gifts, we recommend faux furs or textiles. There are fabulous faux fur coats, throws and shawls.

Gifts for Her

A faux fur jacket

Gifts for Him

A new suit, fur-lined gloves

Fourteenth Year

~Traditional~

Originally, ivory was the traditional gift for 14th wedding anniversaries but was modified to animals once the cruelty of the ivory industry was exposed.

Gifts for Her

A donation to a local animal shelter, horseback riding

Gifts for Him

A safari, a puppy

~Modern~

As such a valuable metal, gold jewelry shows your spouse how much they are worth to you.

Gifts for Her

A gold bracelet

Gifts for Him

A gold tie clip

15th Year

~Traditional~

Crystal is the first costly gift of the traditional items. The investment of time deserves the investment of money!

Gifts for Her

Crystal champagne flutes, crystal frame with a photo of you together

Gifts for Him

A crystal decanter

~Modern~

The investment of time deserves the investment of money. This gift celebrates your years together – and to many more!

Gifts for Her

A watch

Gifts for Him

A watch

20th Year

~Traditional~

China is fragile just like love. It requires care and serves as a reminder to not take a marriage for granted.

Gifts for Her

An updated set of China

Gifts for Him

A trip to China

~Modern~

Platinum is a strong metal that endures just as a 20-year marriage has endured the test of time.

Gifts for Her

A platinum ring with your wedding date

Gifts for Him

An engraved platinum flask

25th Year

~Traditional~

Silver is a precious metal and is prized the world over. Remember to value marriage and allow the relationship to shine like the surface of this metal.

Gifts for Her

Engraved silver jewelry, silver flatware, a silver frame

Gifts for Him

Silver cuff-links, silver money clip

~Modern~

Silver is a precious metal and is prized the world over. Remember to value marriage and allow the relationship to shine like the surface of this metal.

Gifts for Her

Engraved silver jewelry, silver flatware, a silver frame

Gifts for Him

Silver cuff-links, silver money clip

30th Year

~Traditional~

A pearl is a treasured gem, hidden in the shell of an oyster. The pearl represents peace and beauty. Another valuable gem, diamonds, also symbolize great beauty.

Gifts for Her

A pearl necklace, a mother-of-pearl vase

Gifts for Him

A seafood dinner, a snorkeling adventure to find your own pearls

~Modern~

Another valuable gem, the diamond, also symbolizes great beauty.

Gifts for Her

Dazzling diamond earrings

Gifts for Him

Tickets to see Earth, Wind, and Fire, Neil Diamond, etc.

35th Year

~Traditional~

In ancient societies, coral was said to protect from sickness and harm. May this gift bring you health and safety!

Gifts for Her

A coral necklace, nautical themed gifts

Gifts for Him

A trip to the Great Barrier Reef

~Modern~

Jade was once used as a form of currency in Chinese culture and is now considered a symbol of luck.

Gifts for Her

A jade bracelet, a jade vase

Gifts for Him

A jade tie clip, a mini jade desk statue

40th Year

~Traditional~

The red ruby symbolizes love and passion. Keep the flames of marriage burning.

Gifts for Her

Ruby red roses, ruby earrings, a red scarf

Gifts for Him

A case of his favorite red wine, a visit to the ruby mines in North Carolina

~Modern~

The red ruby symbolizes love and passion. Keep the flames of marriage burning.

Gifts for Her

Ruby red roses, ruby earrings, a red scarf

Gifts for Him

A case of his favorite red wine, a visit to the ruby mines in North Carolina

45th Year

~Traditional~

As the stone of royalty, sapphire is a worthy way of celebrating a monumental anniversary!

Gifts for Her

A sapphire necklace, a deep blue crystal bowl, a sapphire bracelet

Gifts for Him

An exotic cruise, a sapphire blue cashmere sweater

~Modern~

As the stone of royalty, sapphire is a worthy way of celebrating a monumental anniversary!

Gifts for Her

A sapphire necklace, a deep blue crystal bowl, a sapphire bracelet

Gifts for Him

An exotic cruise, a sapphire blue cashmere sweater

50th Year

~Traditional~

Gold is the most prized metal and 50 years together should be celebrated with a most prized possession.

Gifts for Her

A gold necklace, a heart-shaped pendant

Gifts for Him

A gold tie clip, a gold nugget, a gold watch

~Modern~

Gold is the most prized metal and 50 years together should be celebrated with a most prized possession.

Gifts for Her

A gold necklace, a heart-shaped pendant

Gifts for Him

A gold tie clip, a gold nugget, a gold watch

60th Year

~Traditional~

In Greek, the word diamond means unconquerable. After 60 years together you have proven your relationship is unconquerable, which deserves the most magnificent gem.

Gifts for Her
A diamond ring to celebrate your life together, a diamond brooch

Gifts for Him
Diamond cufflinks, a trip to Washington, D.C. to see the Hope Diamond

~Modern~

In Greek, the word diamond means unconquerable. After 60 years together you have proven your relationship is unconquerable, which deserves the most magnificent gem.

Gifts for Her
A diamond ring to celebrate your life together, a diamond brooch

Gifts for Him
Diamond cufflinks, a trip to Washington, D.C. to see the Hope Diamond

Love Stories &
Romantic Ideas

I promised you real life love stories, and this one's amazing and heaven sent!

There was a woman on her way to work. She worked at an office building downtown but was slightly late. Since her office building was on the 5th floor, she usually took the stairs for morning exercise. This particular morning, she decided to ride the elevator. When she stepped on the elevator there was a gentleman getting on at the same time. They had never seen one another before, but after a short conversation they realized that they worked at two different companies in the same building. Before the man got off on the third floor where he worked, he asked her out on a date for later that evening. They went on the date, and it was an instant connection. They were married the same week and have been happily married for 20 years.

Here's a set-up that sounds more like a Saturday Night Live skit than a rom com, but it's 100% true.

Deborah and Carlo Pann met in 1978 when they were both contestants on the game show "Jeopardy!" It was a meet cute with a musical twist. It turns out they were the only two contestants to successfully identify the longest song title of an ASCAP record: "How Could You Believe Me When I Said I Loved You, When You Know I've Been A Liar All My Life?" originally sung by Fred Astaire and Jane Powell in the 1951 musical Royal Wedding. Fortunately, that song title didn't set the stage for a rocky romance. A few weeks later, they started dating, and within a few years, they were married. Today they have two grown sons, and they still yell at the TV together when they watch "Jeopardy!"

Now that's what we call full circle!

A Tire Change that Changed Her Life!

I heard a particular Pastor share this beautiful love story about how a woman met her husband. One thing I remember most about this true love story is that she seemed happy, especially when she talked about her husband. It was clear; she was smitten with him. The way they met was quite unusual. What's even more unusual was that it was love at first sight for them both. He was a bachelor who had been asking God for the right moment to happen so when he found his soul mate, he knew she would be his wife. It was a dark and rainy night, just like you might see in the movies. This woman was driving home from work when she hit a pothole and her tire ruptured. Fortunately, she could pull to the side of the road safely. Unfortunately, this happened before the age of cell phones. That meant all she could do was sit in her car on the side of the road as it listed toward the tire that was missing a chunk of rubber and most of its air. She cautiously emerged from her car and checked the trunk for a spare tire. In the trunk, she found a spare tire—full-sized, not those mini donuts cars come with now—and a tire jack. It was too bad she had never learned how to change a car tire. Just when she thought about walking home in the dark, a car pulled up behind her, and a man stepped out into the rain. After changing the tire, the woman asked how much she owed him for the tire change, he replied, "it was an honor to help someone in need during this time of distress." However, he asked her out on a date. Months later after the couple dated, they were married. The woman always thanked God for sending her knight in shining armor, and the man always thanked God for finding his good thing and divine favor.

They are still happily married to this day.

First Date Ideas

First Date Ideas to Help Spark a Love Connection (or at Least a Great Time)

When my significant other and I first started dating, a lot of our date nights ended up in one of two ways. The first was a night out with dinner, drinks, and ordering Ubers, which left us diving deeper into our budgets than we preferred. The second was laying horizontally, spending a grueling 35 minutes trying to decide on a feature to watch, then falling asleep minutes into the intro of a movie we had already seen. Our latest and greatest solution? Brainstorming cheap date ideas that would keep us entertained (and vertical) without breaking the bank.

Dating your significant other, no matter how long you've been together, is a perfect (and necessary) opportunity to reset, connect, and fall in love all over again. In the spirit of keeping things fresh without compromising your finances, here are 10 cheap date night ideas for times when you want a middle ground between binge watching Netflix and splurging on dinner and drinks downtown:

1. Just do dinner!

There's a reason a dinner date is a classic. With no distractions other than something delicious, dinner is a great way to bond with a new potential partner.

2. Cook together.

Go on a grocery run together and whip up something yummy. You'll get to know one another through the process and be able to enjoy the fruits of your labors together.

3. Go for a stroll

It's so simple but walking side by side can actually help quell some of the anxiety and awkwardness usually associated with first date conversation. (This is also a great option for long-term couples who need to open their lines of communication!)

4. Walk shelter dogs

Of course, if one of you is allergic this is a no-go, but it's a great way to get to know each other, do a good deed, and see how your potential partner responds to a cute pooch. We all know dogs are great judges of character, so consider this part of the vetting process!

5. Get breakfast

Does dinner feel like too much pressure? Opt for the ultimate comfort food: Pancakes.

6. Make a sweet deal

Get out for some dessert! Hit up a local bakery, candy or ice cream shop and treat yourselves to something sweet.

7. Bust out the board games

A little friendly rivalry is a great way to break the ice, whether it's Monopoly, Taboo, Scattergories or good old Chutes n) Ladders.

8. Hit up an arcade

Whether you battle each other in Street Fighter or work together to beat a side-scroller, bonding over video games is a great way to garner laughs and bond.

9. Make it a movie night

Even if you're not too keen to return to physical movie theaters just yet, you can still recreate the experience at home. Make a tub of popcorn, bust out some Twizzlers and pick out something new On Demand or streaming.

10. Have a karaoke night (out or at home)

Find out their favorite songs and belt them out. Bonus points if you guys' duet!

11. Go for a swim

Whether you live by water, have a pool or just live near a hotel that does, taking a dip can be a great time.

12. Hit up a library or bookstore

Pick out books for one another and you'll have something to discuss on date two!

13. Build something great together

Whether it's a Lego project or a 2,000-piece puzzle, working together towards a common goal is a great way to connect.

14. Go bowling

A tried-and-true classic date for a reason: It's low-pressure enough where you'll just get goofy, and if you're that bad at it, just add bumpers and laugh.

15. Play ping-pong

Find a local ping-pong club or just set up a net on your coffee table.

16. Go skating

Whether a roller ring or on ice, there's something about maintaining one's center of gravity that just screams romance.

17. Visit a zoo

Seeing cute critters will make you both happy, and there are few better icebreakers than wild animals.

18. Go to an art gallery

Whether you're an art aficionado or just like coloring books, strolling around and perusing some paintings is a great way to kill time and open discussions.

19. Tour a botanical garden or park

Life is great when you literally stop to smell the roses together.

20. Enjoy an aquarium

Ooh and ahh at the fish, dolphins and aquatic life together.

21. Go on a picnic

Outdoor dining may well be your safest option right now. Grab a blanket, pack some snacks and head to your favorite park.

22.　Shoot hoops

Get sweaty with a friendly game of HORSE or one-on-one.

23.　Shoot pool

Billiards is a great time and gives you both plenty of opportunity to chat.

24.　Play laser tag

It's dark, it's silly and you can either work as a team or compete against each other and still have a great time.

25.　Go for a bike ride

Stop for lunch or a snack and explore your 'hood.

About the Author

Christopher W. Strahan is Overseer & Founder of Tree of Life Outreach Ministries, International, Pastor of Circle of Life Interdenominational Christian Center, Leader of Coalition of Truckers In Christ, Public Relations of Lives Ever Revolving Media Network, Business Owner of promo IMPACT, Assured Force Security Technology and Author of the book titled, "Phenomenal Lover" in Baton Rouge, LA. GOD has Blessed and Gifted him in ministry where there is a True Divine Guidance of The Holy Spirit, impartation, worship, preaching, teaching, healing, deliverance, prophecy and soul winning for Christ! Chris was born in Jackson, Mississippi on August 20, 1972, and raised by a single parent, his mother Brenda L. Strahan. He is the only child she birthed. Chris's father is Wayne K. Hampton in Baton Rouge, LA. He himself is also a proud father. The vision that GOD has given Chris is to be an instrument of GOD that brings together numerous ministries in a concerted team effort to accomplish the goal of world evangelism on quest in search of winning people for Christ. Chris is a qualified Evangelist, Pastor, and Minister of the Gospel called to the 5-Fold Ministry with licenses and credentials for ministry, issued by Pastor J.M. LaMotte, Sr. of New Saints In Christ Community Outreach Ministries and the State of Louisiana on October 28th, 2010. Chris is no stranger to ministry, because he was called and chosen by GOD to Preach the Gospel on December 31, 1993. Having spent a combination of 23 years with several positions which include, a Deacon, Minister, Youth Vice President, Poet, Gospel Rapper, Men's Group Leader, and Outreach Pastor. Chris is also the radio host of "Lives Ever Revolving." Chris hosted a major Conference, "MARRIED, DIVORCED, AND SINGLE CONFERENCE," at the Florida Parishes Event Arena Center in Amite City, LA, with the radio owner of WABL 1570AM AND 97.3FM Ericka "Lady T" Taylor, in which both broadcasts Chris currently hosts.

www.ingramcontent.com/pod-product-compliance
Lightning Source LLC
Chambersburg PA
CBHW050412030726
47503CB00006B/2155